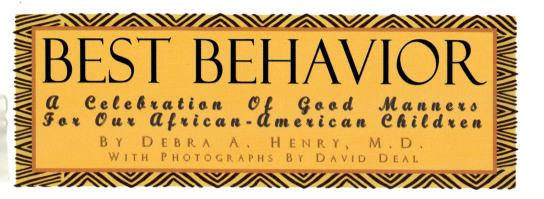

Copyright © 2004 by Debra A. Henry, M.D.
All rights reserved. No part of this book may be reproduced in whole or in part without prior written permission from the publisher.

Inquiries should be addressed to:
Black Society Pages, Inc.
P.O. Box 19522
Alexandria, Virginia 22320

Library of Congress Control Number 2004094315
ISBN 0-9758611-0-7

Black Society Pages, Inc.
Alexandria, Virginia
www.blacksocietypages.com

Introduction

Etiquette and psychiatry are a curious pairing. The medical profession has trained me to focus on pathology rather than wellness, on what is bad rather than what is good, on what is broken rather than what works. This background has prepared me to attempt to solve problems that I encounter in my medical practice and in daily living. With this goal in mind, I have written several poems designed to guide our children towards proper etiquette and behavior.

While psychiatry seeks to diagnose and treat behavioral problems, etiquette is a refinement of common conduct that has its own boundaries and proprieties. Although many societal changes have occurred since the Civil Rights Movement of the 50s and 60s, the "me generation" of the 70s and 80s, and the Hip Hop culture of the 90s and beyond, basic codes of conduct for African-Americans remain unchanged.

Our African-American children are the products of their environments. Their parents, teachers, clergy and peers and the advertisement and entertainment media shape their behaviors. Many societal and cultural influences tend to negate the values that families try to instill. Through poetry and photographs, this book attempts to inform and to reinforce some core principles of decorum for young children. Perhaps, the vocabulary utilized in this book may challenge little listeners or readers; however, it is my hope that the subject will interest and stimulate them to learn more about the lexicon as well as etiquette. My writing is not a psychological or pathological approach to manners. Rather, it is a celebration and affirmation of appropriate behavior and its rewards. I invite you to celebrate and reaffirm these principles with your family.

In closing, I would like to dedicate this book to my family: to my husband, Vernon, my strength; to my mother, Evelyn, my nurturer; to my father, Thomas, my teacher; to my son, Ross, my inspiration. I appreciate your support and am grateful for your love. Thank you!

Debra A. Henry, M.D.

Contents

Best Behavior	4
Common Courtesies	6
Sorry	8
The Handshake	10
Confidence	12
Excuse Me	14
Thank You	16
Excellence	18
Interruptions/Mind Your Business	20
Table Manners	22
Please	24
Bad Words	26
Titles and Surnames	28
Character	30

Best Behavior

The art of good manners
Is called Etiquette.
Rules and Tools,
You should not forget.

Respect for others
Is the cornerstone.
Disruptive deportment
Should not be condoned.

It makes no sense to be
Surly or rude.
Possess a kind spirit
And a nice attitude.

A positive outlook
Will go a long way,
Along with something
Pleasant to say.

Regarding demeanor,
Neatness does count.
Practice good conduct
In generous amounts.

Little Children of Africa,
A key to success
Is to be well mannered
And behave your best.

Common Courtesies

Pulling out your chair,
Opening your door,
Picking up your book,
When it falls on the floor.

All of these actions
Are common courtesies.
I do them for you and
You do them for me.

You should not expect payment,
Or something in return,
But if you hear "Thank you,"
Know that gratitude is well earned.

Sorry

If you do something
That you regret,
You should seek forgiveness,
Without fuss or fret.

For a deed that is done,
Take responsibility.
Good or bad, happy or sad,
Do not show hostility.

Ask for a pardon.
Have no hard feelings.
Please express your sorrow
In these difficult dealings.

Apologies, though necessary,
Are sometimes hard to say.
Merely say "I'm Sorry"
If things don't go your way.

The Handshake

Shaking hands is what you do,
When you meet
Someone new.

Look the person in the eye.
Extend your hand,
Don't be shy.

With a firm grip,
You will shake.
Honest, true, never fake.

If goodwill
You want to show,
A handshake
Is the way to go.

Confidence

I am Pretty,
The Smartest,
The Best.
I am Handsome,
Better than the rest.

Just because I know it,
I don't have to show it.
I don't have to say it
In order to convey it.

To brag or boast
Is a sure sign of insecurity.
Do not show off.
Be confident!
That's true maturity.

Excuse Me

Passing gas is normal.
It is not done for show.
Every person does it
From above or below.

It is not the bad smells
Or the loud sounds
(The cause may be indigestion)
But what a person does in the end
That may raise a question.

Just say "Excuse me."
No proclamation to be made.
Those two little words
Will bring you favor
Until the odor fades.

Thank You

You can say thank you
by a thoughtful display:
In a card,
With a gift,
By a flower bouquet.

You can be thankful
by your good mood:
Be appreciative,
Be gracious,
Have a polite attitude.

When you say thank you,
you will express:
Kindness,
Gratitude,
And Happiness.

So be thankful everyday
And you will be blessed
In so many ways!

Excellence

If I exhibit good conduct,
They say I "act white."
Is there something wrong
With being polite?

If I do well in school,
They call me a "nerd,"
As if academic achievement is
Something absurd.

If I speak Standard English,
No slang I do use.
I am laughed at, made fun of,
Teased and abused.

If I am a leader,
Not following the crowd,
I must stand by myself and
Singled out, I am proud.

The epitome of excellence
Is our legacy.
Success is our birthright,
For you and for me.

Is the best that life offers
For Caucasians alone?
As African-Americans,
All things excellent are our own.

Interruptions

Interruptions are unpleasant.
Interruptions are not fun.
Interruptions are a bother.
They can make one feel undone.

No interrupting when conversing
With your family and friends.
Just take your time.
Please wait your turn
Until the speaker ends.

Mind Your Business

Mind Your Business.
Do Not Dip.
No Eavesdropping.
No Loose Lips.

Listen Not
Unless Spoken To.
What You Hear
May Not Be For You.

Table Manners

My elbows are off the table.
I sit straight in my chair.
I do not want to make a mess,
Eating meals with so much care.

Using proper utensils,
Spoon and knife on the right.
My fork is on the left,
My grace I do recite.

Never talking with my mouth full,
I chew slowly with small bites.
Making pleasant conversation,
I am cheerful and polite.

Table manners are important.
They are a must to know.
To use them is essential,
I will practice them as I grow.

Please

If you want someone to do
Something for you,

If you wish they would share,
Show them you care.

If you have a request,
Stand out from the rest.

If there is an object you crave,
Don't rant or rave.

No orders, no commands,
No threatening demands,

No hate, nor hostility,
Inquire with civility.

Don't say it too late.
Just ask and appreciate.

You may say it with ease.
Simply say "Please!"

Bad Words

I can't believe what I have heard!
"Oh! You said a bad word!"

Foul language is obscene,
A way to be hurtful,
A way to be mean,
A negative form of "acting out,"
Crude behavior without a doubt.

To express what you have to say
There is always a better way.
This type of language has no use,
Cursing is a poor excuse.

Dirty words,
They do offend.
So say you're sorry
And make amends.

Titles and Surnames

Mr., Mrs., Ms., and Miss
Are titles for grown-ups.
Calling your elders by first names?
Did you forget?
Adults are not your peers.
You are not old enough yet!

Mrs. Brown and Mr. White,
Use their last names.
It is only right!
Miss Sally and Ms. Suzie will do,
If they are well known to you!

Mr., Mrs., Ms., and Miss
Are titles for grown-ups.
Use titles and surnames.
Do not forget.
While you are young,
You should show much respect!

Character

Character is
The person you are,
The traits you cannot see
Neither near nor far.

It is not the color of your skin
Nor the curl of your hair.
It is the things about you
that are invisibly there.

Kindness, Honesty, and Responsibility;
Self-respect, Thoughtfulness, and Integrity;
Modesty, Politeness, and Reliability;
Goodness, Wholesomeness and Dignity.

These qualities of a person
Are evident in all that you say and do.
These characteristics
Are uniquely *YOU!*

Give The Gift Of BEST BEHAVIOR
To Your Family And Friends

Form of Payment: ☐ Check ☐ Visa ☐ MasterCard

$ _____ Amount included for _____ (quantity) copies of BEST BEHAVIOR at $12.95 each

$ _____ Virginia residents must include 5% sales tax

$ _____ All orders must include $3 for shipping and handling

$ _____ If ordering more than one book, include $1 per book for each additional book

$ _____ Total amount included or to be charged to credit card

Name _____

Organization _____

Address _____

City/State/Zip _____

Phone _____

Email _____

Card Number _____

Exp. Date ___ ___ / ___ ___ Signature _____

Make your check payable and return this form to:
Black Society Pages, Inc.
P.O. Box 19522
Alexandria, Virginia 22320

If you are paying by credit card, you may fax this form to (703) 642-8039
Or order online at www.blacksocietypages.com
Special discounts are available for group orders
For more information, please contact: info@blacksocietypages.com